OTHER BOOKS IN THE AFTER-SCHOOL
SUPERSTARS SERIES

NIXIE NESS
COOKING STAR

VERA VANCE
COMICS STAR

AFTER-SCHOOL SUPERSTARS

★★LUCY LOPEZ★★
CODING STAR

Claudia Mills

pictures by Grace Zong

MARGARET FERGUSON BOOKS
HOLIDAY HOUSE · NEW YORK
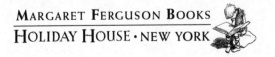

Margaret Ferguson Books
HOLIDAY HOUSE is registered in the U.S. Patent and Trademark Office.
Printed and bound in August 2020 at Maple Press, York, PA, U.S.A.
www.holidayhouse.com
First paperback edition, 2020
1 3 5 7 9 10 8 6 4 2
Library of Congress Cataloging-in-Publication Data
Names: Mills, Claudia, author. | Zong, Grace, illustrator.
Title: Lucy Lopez, coding star / Claudia Mills ; pictures by Grace Zong.
Description: First edition. | New York : Holiday House, [2020]
Series: After-school superstars | "Margaret Ferguson Books."
Audience: Ages 7-10 | Audience: Grades 2-3 | Summary: Third-grader
Lucy Lopez attends coding camp at her after-school program
and becomes a coding star.
Identifiers: LCCN 2019036535 | ISBN 9780823446285 (hardcover)
Subjects: CYAC: Computer programming—Fiction.
After-school programs—Fiction. | Schools—Fiction.
Classification: LCC PZ7.M63963 Lr 2020 | DDC [Fic]—dc23
LC record available at https://lccn.loc.gov/2019036535
ISBN: 978-0-8234-4628-5 (hardcover)
ISBN: 978-0-8234-4921-7 (paperback)

★

*To my beloved sister, Cheryl Mills,
who made the Let's Have Fun Club with me,
and to all younger sisters everywhere*

★

LUCY LOPEZ

CODING STAR

★ one ★

Lucy Lopez poked her older sister, Elena, who sat hunched over the keyboard in front of the family-room computer. On the screen a kangaroo was dancing to a hip-hop beat. The kangaroo kicked to the right, kicked to the left, then twirled in place, paws waving.

Of course a kangaroo would dance to hip-hop.

"You've been on the computer *forever*," Lucy complained. If only Elena would finish up and work on their special club badges with her instead. But ever since Elena had attended a four-week after-school coding camp a month ago with her best friend, Juniper, it was hard to tear her away from the computer.

Elena ignored Lucy's comment. With another few motions of her busy fingers on the touchpad, Elena had changed the code to make the dancing kangaroo a dancing hedgehog, hopping just as energetically.

"Mom said only one hour," Lucy pointed out.

"Yes, and I still have one minute and forty-seven seconds left," Elena replied, glancing at the timer on the table.

Elena paused the dance to turn the hedgehog into a turtle moving jerkily like a robot, and then—hooray, hooray!—only five seconds were left on the timer—four, three, two, one, *ding*!

"*Now* let's work on our badges!" Lucy said.

She and Elena had created a special sisters' club after their mother announced she was done forever with any activities that involved anybody having to sell anything: wrapping paper, coupon books, or—especially—cookies. So Lucy and Elena had made the Let's Have Fun Club, where they created their own badges, designing what each badge looked like in a Let's Have Fun Club handbook, and making up lists of the things they had to do to earn each one. Once they earned a badge, they cut it out of the handbook and taped it onto a crepe-paper sash.

The club name was perfect because earning badges was the most fun thing in the entire world. So far they had earned badges for making bracelets, reading books, and completing jigsaw puzzles. The jigsaw-puzzle badge was Lucy's favorite. She was the one who had made up its list of requirements:

1. Finish three 100-piece puzzles.

2. Finish one 500-piece puzzle all by yourself with no help from anyone else.

3. Do five 25-piece little-kid puzzles in under five minutes.

4. Do one little-kid puzzle with the pieces turned picture-side down.

5. Make your own puzzle by pasting a picture from a magazine onto cardboard and cutting it up into jigsaw-puzzle pieces.

But these days all Elena wanted to do was

sit at the computer and code, code, code—even though the hair-styling badge they were supposed to be working on was one Elena herself had created.

"All right," Elena said reluctantly, pushing her chair back from the computer. "I'll show you how to make those cute little double buns, one on each side of your head. That's number four on the list of badge requirements."

Ten minutes later, both girls had two dark knobs of hair sticking up on the tops of their heads, like extra pairs of fuzzy black-bear ears. When they inspected themselves in the bathroom mirror, Lucy could see the buns Elena had made on Lucy's head were neater than the buns Lucy had made on Elena's head.

"Are mine good enough for the badge?" Lucy asked.

Sometimes Elena was extra-picky about the badges. She hadn't let Lucy count one of her bracelets for the bracelet-making badge since she had copied Elena's design too closely.

"Sure," Elena said. "Our handbook doesn't say 'Make a *perfect* double bun.' Messy buns are in right now, anyway."

Lucy let out her breath with happy relief. "Now can we make French braids?" she asked. "It's the only thing we have left for the badge."

Elena shook her head. "That's enough club stuff for today. I'm going over to Juniper's for a while." In a whisper she added, "*Her* mom doesn't put a timer on *her* computer."

So ten minutes later, Elena was gone and Lucy was alone. She could start working on earning a different badge from the handbook—like the cookie-baking badge—but she and Elena had always earned their badges together. It wouldn't be the same baking cookies all by herself.

Maybe they could create a coding badge for the club! And Elena could show Lucy how to write codes for it, the way she had shown her how to make the double buns. But for some reason, Elena never wanted to show Lucy how to do stuff on the computer. Of course, it would take a lot longer to teach someone how to do computer coding than to teach them how to make a new hairstyle. Elena had spent a whole month in coding camp to learn everything she knew now.

What if . . . what if Lucy went to coding camp, too? Lucy had a flyer stuffed in the bottom of her backpack for a third-grade coding camp run by the same teachers who had taught Elena's fifth-grade camp. If Lucy went to coding camp, she'd learn the things Elena already knew without having to nag Elena, and then she and Elena could earn a Let's Have Fun Club coding badge together!

Lucy found her mother on the couch in the family room, red pen in hand, grading Spanish quizzes. Looking up from her pile of papers, her mother focused her gaze on Lucy's head.

"What are *those*?"

"Double buns. Elena made them for me."

"Oh," her mother said. "Fancy."

"Can I go to coding camp?" Lucy asked. "Like Elena did? The one for third graders starts this week."

She held out the crumpled flyer she had retrieved from the bottom of her backpack.

Her mother gave a huge sigh. "Well, fair is fair," she said.

Lucy had expected the sigh. In addition to disapproving of programs that involved selling things, her mom thought kids nowadays had too many scheduled activities. So most days after school Lucy and Elena walked across the elementary-school parking lot to the high school, where their mom taught Spanish and their dad taught history. There they did homework or read books until it was time for everyone to go home. Elena had used her best begging skills to convince their mom to let her do the coding camp.

"It's just that . . . everything's a camp or a class nowadays," her mother said. "Whatever happened to kids having fun on their own?"

"Elena and I *do* have fun on our own!" They had created a whole entire club to have fun on their own! In fact, the only reason Lucy wanted to go to coding camp was because of the club the two of them had created.

"I know," her mother said with another sigh, reaching over to push a stray strand of hair back into one of Lucy's buns. "If you want to do the camp, we'll sign you up."

"Yay!" Lucy nodded so vigorously that one of her buns tumbled down, but she didn't care. "Hooray!"

★ ★ ★

On Sunday afternoon Lucy didn't utter a single complaint as Elena's hour of computer time ticked down. Soon *she'd* be the one with the timer ticking; *her* fingers would be confidently moving on the touchpad; it would be *her* dancing kangaroo!

Now she had a reason to try to follow the blocks flying across the screen to figure out exactly what Elena was doing. How did the kangaroo become a bear? How did the bear know to start doing disco moves? But her sister did everything so quickly, it was still a mystery.

"Stop breathing down my neck," Elena snapped. "Why don't you go get the stuff we need for the French braids? I'll be done in four minutes and twelve—no, eleven—seconds."

French braids turned out to be harder than double buns, and Lucy was so excited about coding camp that she found herself tuning out during some of Elena's instructions. But half an hour later an elegant French braid lay flat against the back of Lucy's head, and a crooked French braid lay flat against the back of Elena's.

"Did I pass?" Lucy asked.

Elena craned her neck around to inspect the braid Lucy had made. She took longer to answer this time.

"Yes," she finally said.

Lucy cut out the circular hair-styling badge from the page in their club handbook where the badges created so far were displayed. Then she promptly taped it to her crepe-paper sash.

She noticed Elena wasn't cutting out her hair-styling badge. In fact, Elena hadn't even added the jigsaw-puzzle badge to her sash yet. Didn't Elena even care about the Let's Have Fun Club anymore?

Was now the time for Lucy to tell Elena she was going to do the coding camp, too, so they could start earning Let's Have Fun Club coding badges together? Maybe that would make Elena excited about the club the way she used to be.

But she found herself hesitating. Elena could be so prickly sometimes, like when she hadn't let Lucy count her woven bracelet for the badge because its design wasn't "original" enough. Still, Elena was going to find out about Lucy's coding camp when Lucy didn't walk over to the high school with her tomorrow afternoon.

"I was thinking . . ." Lucy said. "I was thinking that if *I* learned coding, then we could have coding badges for the club, and so I talked to Mom, and she said *I* could go to coding camp, too."

Elena didn't say anything at first, busying herself with gathering up combs and brushes. She collected the rubber bands and returned them to their plastic container. She placed the mirror back in the bathroom vanity drawer.

"I don't think you're going to like coding," Elena said then. "It's really hard. It's not like jigsaw puzzles, where it's super-obvious how the pieces fit together."

Lucy thought a five-hundred-piece jigsaw puzzle was hard. It wasn't obvious how five hundred different pieces fit together.

Elena started unraveling the lopsided French braid Lucy had made for her, yanking at the intertwined strands of hair as if she were mad at them for some reason.

"I just can't see computers being *your* thing," Elena said, "the way they're *my* thing.

You know, like how gardening is Dad's thing, but not Mom's thing? And how salsa dancing is Mom's thing, but not Dad's thing?"

But how could Lucy know if coding was her thing if she had never even tried it?

Then Elena shrugged. "Well, suit yourself. But if you get mega-frustrated with coding, don't come complaining to me."

"I won't," Lucy said.

She didn't plan to be complaining to anybody at all.

Elena didn't understand how fun it would be once she and Lucy could both do cool coding things on the computer for a Let's Have Fun Club coding badge.

Lucy closed her eyes and imagined two sister kangaroos, side by side, happily hip-hopping on the computer screen.

Together.

★ two ★

The after-school coding camp met in one of the third-grade classrooms that wasn't Lucy's. Once the lady-in-charge-of-everything, Colleen, checked her off on the attendance clipboard, Lucy surveyed the space where fifteen or so kids had gathered, hoping to find someone to sit with. Most of the kids were from the other two third-grade classes, but Lucy knew a few of them.

Boogie Bass was always falling out of his chair at lunch in the cafeteria, and then laughing about it afterward. Lucy might as well sit next to him, not that she had ever fallen out of her chair. But if she did, she had a feeling Boogie would grin and make her feel it hadn't been such a catastrophe.

Sure enough, Boogie gave her a big grin as she slipped into her seat.

"You weren't in cooking camp or comic-book camp," he said. "They were awesome, but this one is going to be the awesomest!"

Lucy tried to return his grin. What if coding turned out to be as mega-frustrating for her as Elena had warned it would be?

When all the campers had filed in, Colleen introduced the camp teachers, Preston and Pippa. They looked different from what Lucy had expected. Because they knew everything there was to know about computer coding, Lucy had thought they would look more computer-y—maybe like C-3PO and R2-D2 in *Star Wars*. But they didn't look like robots at all. Preston was short and chubby, like someone who would run a cooking camp. Pippa was tall and slim, with a mane of long flowing curls, like someone who would run an acting camp, maybe even a movie-star camp.

"Okay," Pippa said. "You're here for coding camp. So what is coding?"

It's a way of making kangaroos dance. But

Lucy wasn't going to raise her hand to say that.

Nolan Nanda, who was sitting on the other side of Boogie, was the first with his hand in the air.

"Coding is how people give instructions to a computer so the computer will do what they want it to do," Nolan said in a slow, careful way, more like how Lucy had thought a coding-camp teacher would talk.

"Exactly," Pippa said.

Boogie beamed at Lucy. "Nolan knows everything," he told her proudly.

"Next question," Preston went on. "Are computers smart or dumb?"

"Smart!" most of the campers shouted. Lucy didn't shout anything, but she didn't think computers were very smart if they had to have a person sitting at the keyboard telling them exactly what to do.

Preston and Pippa both shook their heads.

"Nope," Pippa said. As if she didn't want any computers to hear her and feel insulted, she whispered, "Computers are *dumb*." She went on, "Sure, computers can do amazing things. But they can do those things only because some human being told them what to do. In this camp, *you* are going to be that human being."

So Lucy *had* been right! And now *she* would be the human being—just like Elena!

Preston took over. "When you give instructions to a human being, the human being can often figure out what you *meant*, even if it isn't exactly what you *said*. Okay, now I need a human being." He looked around the room and pointed to the girl sitting in front of Nolan. "You. What's your name?"

"Nixie."

"A fine name for a human being! All right, Nixie, please walk around the room."

Nixie giggled as she hopped up from her seat, strutted around the desks and chairs, and then plopped back down into her seat again.

"Ta-da!" Nixie said. "Was I a good human being?"

"You were an excellent human being," Preston said.

Now it was Nixie's turn to beam.

"The rest of you: What are some of the things

Nixie did that a computer wouldn't have known to do because I didn't include those things in my instructions?"

No one raised a hand, not even Nolan. Lucy tried to guess the answer. Well, Nixie had giggled, and a computer wouldn't giggle. And Nixie had walked quickly, and Preston hadn't told her how fast or slow to go.

After a long pause, Preston answered his own question: "She *stood up* first."

That was true! Nixie had also sat down at the end, without being told to do that, either.

Preston seated himself in the teacher's chair and started to "walk" his feet away from the desk, scooting the chair along with him. All the campers laughed, including Lucy.

Then he went on: "Nixie walked around the *perimeter* of the room—the outer edge—instead of just randomly through the desks. But *walk around the room* could just mean walk all over the place, right?"

Now Preston started to "walk" his chair right into the desk of one of the kids sitting in the first row.

"Oops!" Preston said, bumping the kid's

desk, as the campers laughed again. Lucy hadn't expected the computer teachers to be so funny.

"Nixie walked around the room *once*. Did I say to walk around the room just one time? That's exactly what I *intended* for her to do, but it's not what I *told* her to do. But Nixie figured out what I meant because she's a human being, and human beings are smart. Finally, a computer wouldn't even know what a *room* is—or what *walking* is—if we didn't tell it first."

"When do *we* get to start telling stuff to computers?" a kid asked from the back of the room.

Lucy sympathized. Even though everything Preston and Pippa were saying was so interesting, Lucy's fingers itched to start tapping computer keys.

"Soon," Pippa said. "But first we want you to practice thinking the way computers think. So get into small groups—four desks, or maybe five. Each of you, take something you're really good at and try to explain it, step by step, to a group of aliens who just landed here on Earth. The list of steps to do something is called an *algorithm*. The rest of you, pretend to be the aliens, and ask about whatever you don't understand. Got it?"

Lucy knew Boogie and Nolan were best friends, and Nixie was already friends with a quiet girl named Vera. The four of them started pulling their desks together. Pippa had said there could be "maybe five" desks in a group. So Lucy shoved her desk close to the other four and was rewarded by another big grin from Boogie. This time Lucy gave him an equally big grin in return.

"I'll go first," Nixie announced. "What I'm good at is walking a dog."

"I thought you didn't have a dog," Nolan said.

"I don't. But I'd be *great* at walking a dog if I *did* have one. Okay, aliens, first of all, a *dog* is an extremely wonderful kind of *pet*. A *pet* is a special kind of animal that lies in bed with you and loves you better than anyone else in the world. And an *animal* . . ." Nixie started to look worried. "This is going to take forever."

"Just tell us how to *walk* the dog," Vera suggested.

"Okay. First you pick up a *leash*. Do I have to say what a leash is?"

"No!" the others said. It really would take forever to explain absolutely everything to an alien.

Nixie continued, "Stoop down. Then clip the leash on the dog's collar. Then say, 'Come on, boy!' if it's a boy dog, or 'Come on, girl!' if it's a girl dog. Then start walking. I mean, hold on to the leash and start walking toward the door. Open the door. Then close the door. I mean, close the door *after* the dog gets *through* the door, or else you'd squish the dog, which would be terrible. Then keep on walking. Do I have to tell about how to pick up the dog poop if the dog makes a poop?"

"No!" everyone said again.

"So that's how you walk a dog," Nixie concluded. "Did I miss anything?"

"You didn't tell us what *walking* is," Nolan pointed out.

Lucy remembered Preston had said computers would need to have even something this basic explained to them.

"What *walking* is? You guys are really dumb

aliens if you don't even know what walking is. Walking is when you take one step, then another."

"How do you *take a step*?" Nolan asked. He made it sound as if he truly wanted to know.

"You—you—just take a step! Like this!" Nixie got up and demonstrated. "See?"

"We—have—no—eyes," Nolan said in what was clearly a pretend-alien voice. "We—cannot—see."

Nixie's shoulders sagged. "This is too hard!" she wailed.

Lucy felt sorry for her. "Maybe say, move one foot forward one foot. Wait, that sounds totally confusing. So, move your right foot forward twelve inches. Then move your left foot forward twelve inches farther than you moved the right foot. Then move the right foot forward twelve more inches. Then move the left foot."

She felt proud of her explanation of walking, but at the rate she was going, it really would take forever just to explain to an alien how to keep on walking. How *did* anyone walk a dog? It seemed impossible, and yet people did it all the time.

"You can use a loop," Nolan suggested. "That's a coding term for repeating the same sequence of instructions over and over again until you tell it to stop."

Boogie was right: Nolan did know everything. He knew stuff about coding before the coding camp even began. And yes—a loop would solve the problem completely!

Nixie's face brightened. "Okay! Then you do a loop thingy where you keep taking steps forward forever and ever until the dog makes a poop, and then you pick up the poop, and go home again. The end!"

Nolan opened his mouth as if to ask Nixie a few more questions, then shut it.

"Vera, you go next," Nixie said.

Vera furrowed her brow. "I don't think I'm *really* good at anything."

Nixie stared at her. "You're really good at tons of things! Tell an alien how to draw a comic."

Vera shook her head. "That *would* take

forever. And Nolan said aliens can't see. How can you draw something if you can't see what you're drawing?"

"Some aliens can see," Nolan said.

Nixie glared his way. "*Now* you tell me!" But Lucy could tell she was joking.

"Or tell them how to play the piano," Nixie suggested.

"That would take forever, too. Well, maybe I can tell them how to play *Chopsticks*."

Vera did a good job with her explanation, in Lucy's opinion. She had never played the piano herself, but she thought she could play *Chopsticks* now, if she could remember how to find the two white keys right next to each other that started off the piece.

Nolan told the aliens how to shoot a basketball. Apparently his aliens could see, too.

Boogie said, "What I'm best at is being funny, but I don't think I could tell aliens how to be funny. Wait—I could tell them how to lick a quarter and make it stick onto their foreheads. If they have foreheads. And if they have quarters."

Even though everything about the coding camp had been great so far, Lucy felt nervous about her turn. What was she *really* good at? Jigsaw puzzles, maybe, but Elena had acted as if that was a dumb, easy thing to be good at. She loved reading, but the kids in their group knew how to read, so that wouldn't be an interesting thing to explain, even if she could figure out how to explain it. Bracelet making? Elena's rejection of her "copied" bracelet still stung. The only thing left was hair-styling, and she certainly wasn't great at that, either. But she had to say something.

"Okay, aliens," Lucy said, once Boogie's aliens had well-licked coins stuck onto their foreheads. She could hear her voice coming out small and wobbly. "I hope you have hair. Because I'm going to tell you how to make a double bun."

★ three ★

"So how was it?" Lucy's dad asked her, as she buckled herself into the back seat of the car for the ride home from coding camp.

It was wonderful!

Lucy turned toward Elena, who was in the back seat already, gazing out the window as if she had no interest whatsoever in how Lucy answered the question.

She wanted to ask Elena, *Did Preston and Pippa do the same things on the first day of your camp? Did they teach you how to talk to aliens?*

She wanted to tell Elena, *Now I understand why you want to be on the computer all the time. Even talking about coding is tons of fun!*

But something about the stiff way Elena

held her shoulders and looked pointedly in the opposite direction made Lucy hesitate.

Swallowing down her enthusiasm, Lucy said casually, "It was okay."

"Just okay?" her mother asked. "What did you learn so far about coding?"

If she had been alone with her parents in the car, she would have said, *I learned computers are dumb, and aliens are dumb, too, and you have to spell out everything for them, like totally everything. And I did a good job of figuring out how to tell aliens what walking is, and how to make a double hair bun, and I think I might turn out to be good at coding, because I knew some of the answers to the teachers' questions even though I felt too shy to raise my hand and say them.*

But Elena kept staring out the window even though there was nothing to see but the same old walls of their same old elementary school.

Lucy took a deep breath. "I didn't really learn anything. It was just, you know, an introduction kind of day."

With a noisy exhale, Elena turned away

from the window. "It looks like your camp is more basic than mine," she said, sounding relieved. "On our first day, we learned how precise and exact you have to be when you give instructions to computers. Almost like you're talking to aliens who just landed on Earth from outer space. It was supercool."

Now what was Lucy supposed to say?

We learned the same things, and it WAS supercool.

She had a feeling that would be the wrong thing to say.

So she didn't say anything.

Once they returned home, Elena raced inside to start her hour of computer time before setting the table for dinner. Was Lucy going to start having her own hour of computing time now, to do her own coding projects? Well, once she learned how to do them. What would Elena say then? Lucy pushed that thought away.

Lucy and her father lingered in the car for a moment after the others had gone inside. "If you aren't enjoying the coding camp," he told Lucy, "you don't have to do it. Just because Elena loves something doesn't mean you have

to love it, too. It's fine for you and Elena to love different things."

But was it fine for them to love the *same* things?

Apparently not.

"I do like coding camp," Lucy whispered. "I like it a lot."

Her dad raised an eyebrow. She knew she certainly hadn't made it sound as if she liked it.

"Just not as much as Elena," she added, even though Elena wasn't there to hear her.

While Elena was on the computer, Lucy made sure not to loiter behind her chair. Maybe, even though they had always done their badges together, Lucy should make up some new Let's Have Fun Club badges she could earn by herself, without Elena's assistance. Vera could help her earn a piano badge. Nolan could help her earn a basketball badge. Nixie could help her earn a dog-walking badge—if they could find a dog to walk. Boogie could help her earn a magic tricks badge; sticking a quarter on your forehead was sort of like magic.

But most of all, she wanted to earn a coding badge *with* Elena.

After supper both girls went upstairs to read for a while on their matching twin beds in the room they shared.

Before she had even turned the first page, Elena closed her book. "I'm still hungry. Do you want to bake some cookies?"

"Sure!" Lucy said. "We can get started on the cookie-baking badge!"

Elena rolled her eyes, but she hopped up from the bed and was first down the stairs to the kitchen.

The cookie-baking badge had six items on the badge list:

1. Bake chocolate chip cookies because they are the most famous cookies ever.

2. Bake cookies cut out in shapes with cookie cutters. Use at least ten different shapes.

3. Frost a batch of cookies.

4. Make some kind of bar cookies, like brownies or blondies.

5. Make Abuelita's Mexican wedding cookies.

6. Create your own cookie recipe.

Plus, even though the handbook didn't say it, the cookies for the badge had to be made from scratch. You couldn't get a cookie-baking badge for dumping gobs of premade refrigerated dough on a baking sheet and sticking it in the oven for ten minutes.

"So what kind should we make tonight?" Elena asked, as she carried their family recipe box out of the pantry and set it on the kitchen table.

Chocolate chip cookies were definitely the easiest, since they had made them so many times before, though those times didn't qualify because they hadn't been done *for* the badge.

"Chocolate chip!" Lucy announced.

"With nuts?" Elena asked.

It was a joke question: they both loved cookies with nuts.

"Duh!" they said at the same time.

Lucy giggled, and then Elena giggled. Then

they were both laughing "like hyenas." That's what their father called it whenever they laughed hysterically over things he thought weren't even that funny.

As they pulled out the flour and sugar canisters, baking soda, cinnamon, and bags of chocolate chips and chopped walnuts from the pantry shelves, Lucy thought maybe she should have chosen cookie baking to teach the aliens during camp.

She would have had to explain measuring to the aliens: how you scoop the flour into the measuring cup and level it off with the side of a butter knife, but you have to pack the brown sugar in nice and tight. When she told the aliens how to cream the butter together with the brown sugar, she'd have to find a way to let them know when it had been creamed long enough. She could make a loop for the creaming motions, but when exactly would the loop stop?

"If you were telling aliens to keep mixing the dough, using one of those coding loops," she asked Elena, as she was halfway through smushing the butter and sugar together, "how would you tell them when it was mixed enough to stop?"

She remembered too late that this was the wrong question to ask Elena.

Elena's eyes narrowed. "Oh, we didn't learn anything today, it was just introduction stuff," she said, in a high-pitched little-girl voice.

"Well, it was this one boy, Nolan, who told me about the loops," Lucy hastened to explain. "He knows everything there is to know about computers. Coding is definitely *his* thing." Though Boogie had said Nolan knew everything there was to know about everything—so maybe *everything* was Nolan's thing.

Elena broke two eggs to add to the batter. Then Lucy started adding in the flour, baking soda, and salt. As the dough got stiffer and stiffer, Lucy's arm began to ache, but she didn't ask Elena to take a turn, in case Elena was still mad about Lucy's loop question.

Lucy did most of the work dropping the dough in rounded spoonfuls onto the lightly greased baking trays, too; Elena had to text

Juniper to tell her something she had forgotten to tell her at school.

"Ow!" Lucy yelped, as her wrist touched the side of the last tray, hot from the oven. But the cookies did look scrumptious: golden brown, with the chocolate chips still a bit soft and gooey.

"Maybe *baking* is your thing," Elena suggested to Lucy. "Gardening for Dad, dancing for Mom, coding for me, and baking for you."

"Maybe," Lucy said doubtfully.

With her mouth full of warm cookie, she had to admit they had turned out extra-yummy. And it was wonderful to have the first cookie-baking badge requirement crossed off.

But she also had a sore arm, specks of dough in her hair, and a burned wrist.

If it hadn't been for the badge, Lucy would have been just as glad if she had figured out how to give nice clear instructions to the aliens, and they had baked the cookies for her.

★ four ★

"**A**ll right," Pippa told the campers the next day. "Everyone, come and get a notebook."

By "notebook," Lucy saw, Pippa meant a skinny little laptop computer. A computer that would be her very own for the entire month of coding camp. They were even supposed to make sticky labels for them. Lucy wrote her label in big bold letters with hot-pink permanent marker: LUCY LOPEZ.

It was pretty amazing to have a computer with *her* name on it. *Hers!*

It took a long time to hand out the computers and then to write and decorate the labels. Preston and Pippa didn't seem to mind. Lucy's regular classroom teacher, Mrs. Merriweather, was always in a hurry to get another lesson done. One day when they had a fire drill during math time, Lucy had thought Mrs. Merriweather might even burst into tears. But Preston and Pippa acted like they had all the time in the world.

"The more you play, the more you learn," Pippa said. "We're going to be doing a lot of playing this month. You could even call this Computer Play Camp."

That sounded totally fine to Lucy.

Once everyone had logged on to the computer and pulled up the coding website, Preston said, "Yesterday we learned that a list of instructions is called an algorithm. Today we'll be coding, which is turning an algorithm into language the computer can understand. So let's start coding!"

The campers cheered.

The first challenge for the afternoon was to tell a little bunny how to walk down a dock and climb into a sailboat.

The way you told the bunny to do things was with a coding language Pippa called "block coding." Instructions, like *Turn left* or *Move forward,* were printed in little blocks on the left-hand side of the screen. You picked which instructions you wanted to use, dragged them over to the right-hand side of the screen, and clicked them into place.

If you did it right, the bunny would end up on the boat, ready to sail away.

If you did it wrong, the bunny would fall into the water.

You couldn't tell if the bunny was going to be safe and dry on the boat or soaking wet in the ocean until you clicked *Run*, for "run program."

Then the program either worked, or it didn't.

Nolan's program worked right away, of course.

Nixie's, Boogie's, and Vera's didn't.

"My bunny is drowning!" Nixie wailed. Lucy could tell Nixie didn't mind, though. Nixie liked to make everything as dramatic as possible.

"My bunny likes being wet, don't you, bunny?" Boogie said. "He's sort of a fish bunny. Or maybe a fish disguised as a bunny."

Vera kept clicking *Run* over and over again, as if she'd get a different result each time.

SPLASH! She clicked *Run* again. SPLASH! And again. With each SPLASH, Vera looked more and more worried.

Lucy hadn't clicked *Run* yet. If her first, easiest program didn't work, maybe it would mean coding wasn't her thing, just like Elena had said.

"Did yours work?" Nixie asked her.

"I didn't try it," Lucy confessed.

"Lucy!" Nixie stood up and reached over to Lucy's computer touchpad, positioned the cursor on *Run*, and clicked.

As Lucy watched, her heart in her throat, her bunny walked down the dock, turned toward the boat, and then there he was, safe on the deck! Lucy felt like hugging her bunny, even though you couldn't hug a little picture on a computer screen. "You did it!" she whispered to her bunny, even though it was also silly to talk to a little picture on a computer screen.

Actually, Lucy had been the one who had done it. Then again, it had been a very easy puzzle to solve. All the bunny had to do was move forward three times and then turn to the right.

Nixie looked back to her own drowning bunny. "Pippa!" she called. "Preston!"

But Pippa and Preston were busy helping other campers.

"Colleen!" Nixie tried the head camp lady next. Even if Colleen wasn't a coding camp teacher, she was still a grown-up. "My bunny is drowning!"

Colleen gave Nixie a small, sad smile and shook her head. Apparently, rescuing drowning bunnies wasn't part of Colleen's head-camp-lady job. Or else Colleen just wasn't very good at computers. Some grown-ups were terrible at technology. Lucy's dad, who won awards as a history teacher, could barely work the remote on the family TV.

"Campers, help each other!" Pippa called over to their group.

Nolan was already trying to help Vera.

"You can't keep doing the *same* thing," he told Vera, "and expect to get *different* results."

It was just what Lucy had been thinking, but Nolan was more willing to say things out loud than she was.

Right away Nolan figured out that Vera was

telling her bunny to turn left instead of right at the end.

"Try it again," he told Vera, once she changed that one instruction.

Sure enough, Vera's bunny was safe in the boat now, too.

"Nolan to the rescue!" Boogie said. "Nolan, friend to bunnies everywhere!"

As Nolan helped a kid at another desk, who looked even more upset about his drowned bunny than Vera had, Lucy took a peek at Nixie's program. Nixie had told her bunny to move forward too many times. Of course the bunny would run out of dock if it kept walking and walking and walking and walking and walking.

But before she could say anything, Nolan was at Nixie's side. He showed Nixie how to drag some of the *Move forward* commands out of the program.

This time, when Nixie ran the program, her bunny accomplished his mission. "Thanks, Nolan!" Nixie shouted.

Boogie's bunny kept on splashing, but Boogie didn't care.

"My bunny decided not to be a sailor anymore," Boogie announced. "He's going to be a champion swimmer instead. No, a champion *diver*. He *likes* diving into the water. The bigger the splash, the happier he is."

"Coders!" Pippa called out. "Who is ready for the next challenge?"

All hands flew up, even Boogie's.

Pippa showed them how to save their work before going on to the next challenge.

"Good-bye, little bunny," Lucy said as she followed Pippa's instructions.

She thought the bunny might have given her a happy little wave before disappearing.

★ ★ ★

Half an hour later, most of the campers had managed to steer their boats through a maze with a couple of twists and turns in it. This time there was buried treasure waiting at the end. Nolan's boat zoomed over to its treasure. Lucy figured out the puzzle almost as quickly. Nixie was thrilled when her boat finally reached the finish line, with some help from Nolan. Vera's boat got stuck on seaweed; she looked ready to cry until Nolan found a way to make it move forward again. Boogie decided his boat thought it was more fun to bang back and forth forever against the walls of the maze.

Then Preston announced it was time to take a coding break.

"Nooooo!" rose up loud wails from every desk.

"It's good for brains to go outside and get fresh air," Pippa said. "So take yours outside for fifteen minutes and pump some oxygen into them. Believe me, you'll come back ready to solve even harder problems."

"I can't do coding," Vera said, as the girls in Lucy's group followed Colleen outside and drifted over to the playground basketball hoops. Nolan had already sunk one basket, and Boogie was trying—and failing—to bounce a basketball between his legs.

"None of us can do coding!" Nixie told her. "Well, except for Nolan. That's why we're in a coding *camp*. To *learn* how to do it. Besides, you were the best at making comics in the comics camp. You can't be best at *everything*."

Lucy wondered if she was ever going to be

best at *anything*. What would her special thing turn out to be?

Maybe now was the time to ask Nolan to help her get good at basketball so she could start working on a Let's Have Fun Club basketball badge. Maybe she'd turn out to have a talent for basketball she had never discovered before.

She moved closer to the hoop. "Can I play?"

"Sure!" Nolan said.

With a friendly grin, he bounced the basketball toward her, but it came her way too fast for her to be able to catch it. She felt klutzy as she scrambled to pick it up.

"Sorry," Nolan said. "That was a bad pass."

It had been a bad *catch*, but Lucy didn't correct him.

"Can you explain how to shoot a basket again?" Lucy asked. "The way you did when we were pretending to be aliens? But with a real ball now?"

"Sure," Nolan said again.

If an alien can do this, you can, too! Lucy told herself. They had played basketball in P.E. for a couple of weeks last year, and Lucy hadn't been good at it then. But she hadn't wanted to be good at it then as much as she wanted to be good at it now.

She did her best to follow Nolan's careful instructions, but her ball did not soar through the air and go through the hoop. It plunked to the ground a few feet away.

Maybe this was how Vera had felt when she tried to follow the coding instructions but her boat got stuck in the seaweed.

On Lucy's next try, the ball soared too high, way over the top of the backboard.

Even imaginary aliens would do better than this!

Just then Preston's voice rang out from the door opening onto the playground. "Calling all coders! Back inside, everyone!"

Boogie ran to retrieve Lucy's ball, but when he tossed it her way, she missed the ball again, and it bonked her on the side of her head.

At least if you coded a computer basketball game, and you got the program wrong, you wouldn't get bonked with the ball!

Whatever Lucy's special thing might be, she was pretty sure it wasn't basketball.

★ five ★

Pippa hadn't been joking when she said the camp should be called Computer Play Camp. She and Preston offered new coding challenges every day and gave tips for how to solve them. One day they talked about loops, which Lucy's group already knew about from Nolan. But most of the camp time was spent playing with coding puzzles on their own.

On Friday, Preston began camp by saying, "Today we're going to talk about *if* and *then*."

Some kids laughed. It did sound like a strange thing to talk about. What could anyone possibly say about *if*?

"The words *if* and *then* connect two events," Preston went on. "*If* the first one happens, *then* the second one happens, too. When those things don't happen, something *else* does."

Lucy still didn't understand. She saw plenty of other blank faces, too. Only Nolan nodded. Of course Nolan would be the one to nod. If a question was asked, then Nolan knew the answer.

Maybe that was what Preston was talking about?

If a question was asked, *then* Nolan knew the answer.

"So," Preston continued, "*if* it rains this afternoon, *then* you'll have your brain break indoors in our classroom. Or *else*, we'll send you outside. Computer coding is full of *if-then-else* commands, called 'conditionals,' which we'll talk about in a few minutes. But *life* is full of them, too. Share some ideas with your buddies."

Nixie went first in their group. "*If* I get a dog, *then* I'll be happy forever. What am I supposed to say for the *else* thing?"

Nolan helped her out. "Or *else*, you'll keep asking until your wish comes true. Okay, here's mine: *If* Nixie gets a dog, *then* the rest of us will be happy forever. Or *else*, we'll have to listen to her complaining for all eternity."

Nixie grinned at Nolan.

"*If* you get a dog, *then* you'll have to walk it," Boogie warned her.

"I'll *want* to walk it," Nixie replied.

"That's what you think now," Boogie said darkly.

"*If* Nixie gets a dog, *then* I'll help her walk it," Vera promised.

Lucy had been thinking, If *I want to get good at coding,* then *I'm going to need to practice coding on the computer at home.* Or else, *I'll never be able to make a kangaroo dance like Elena does.* She had already asked her mom about having her own hour of computer time, and her mom had said, as Lucy knew she would, *Well, fair is fair.* But would this make Elena get sniffy and crabby?

Lucy didn't want to think about that now. Instead she just said, "*If* Nixie gets a dog, *then* I'll help her walk it, too."

Maybe she really could get a dog-walking badge. The badge requirements could be: walk a dog, pick up dog poop, go running with a dog, play fetch with a dog, and take a dog to a dog park. Of course, step one would be: find a dog to walk.

Pippa next explained how conditionals were used in coding. If you were trying to steer a boat through a maze, the way they had been doing, you could plan ahead for what the boat should do depending on which way the maze turned, rather than having to code each twist and turn separately.

If the path turned right, *then* turn the boat to the right. Or *else*, the boat continues to go straight.

If the path turned left, *then* turn the boat to the left. Or *else*, the boat continues to go straight.

That sounded pretty clear to Lucy.

"Okay, coders, steer the boat!" Preston told them.

★ ★ ★

Fifteen minutes later, Vera sat slumped in front of her computer, staring at the screen as if she could propel her boat through the watery maze with her eyeballs.

"I think my computer is broken," she said.

Lucy shot Vera a sympathetic glance. Computers did break, usually at the worst

possible time. She often heard her mother saying angry things in Spanish to the computer at home when she was trying to enter grades for her students. But somehow she didn't think Vera's computer was broken this time.

"I think my *boat* is broken," Boogie said. "Or maybe it just likes crashing into walls. Maybe a computer-game company will hire me to create a game called *Shipwreck*. The winner is the person whose ship gets wrecked first. Or most. Or worst."

Vera didn't smile.

"You're not even *trying*," she told Boogie. "But I am. And the more I try, the worse it gets. And *my* ship does *not* like being wrecked. It *hates* it!"

As Nolan started helping Vera figure out what was wrong with her code, Lucy looked over from her screen to his. Her program had twelve steps in it; his had eight. Both of them had gotten their boat through the maze without crashing, but he had done it faster.

Once Vera's boat was on its way again, Lucy pointed this out to Nolan. "Your code is shorter than mine. Is shorter better?"

"Remember when Nixie was teaching the aliens how to walk a dog?" Nolan asked.

Lucy nodded. That would have been hard to forget.

"And how glad we were when she figured out how to shorten the instructions? Coding is sort of like that. But your code worked great, Lucy. All your codes have worked great."

Lucy was surprised Nolan had noticed. He must be a very noticing kind of person. It felt good to get a coding compliment from someone who was so great at coding himself.

"Anyway," Nolan went on, "the cool thing is that there's never just one solution for a problem. There're always different ways to solve any problem."

"What different ways are there to solve *my* problem?" Nixie asked him.

Nolan gazed over at her screen.

"Not *that* problem! My *real* problem! The problem of how to get a *dog*!"

"Well," Nolan said slowly, as if he was already working out an algorithm for "how to get a dog" in his head. "You could *find* a dog.

You could *buy* a dog. You could *adopt* a dog from a shelter."

"But my parents won't let me!" Nixie protested. "They say dogs cost too much and are too much work."

"Or you could *borrow* a dog," Nolan finished.

"You could borrow *my* dog," Boogie offered. "You could walk him every single day. I'll give you extra-big poop bags, too."

Nixie's face lit up, as if she had been dreaming of extra-big poop bags all her life. "Do you mean it?"

"Cross my heart." Boogie made a crossing motion that was more over his stomach than his heart, in Lucy's opinion.

Nixie turned to Vera and Lucy, the two who had said, If *Nixie gets a dog,* then *I'll help her walk it.*

"Did you mean it, too?"

"Well," Vera said uncomfortably. "It was more that I had to say *something* with *if-then* in it. I'm not a dog person. But I *do* want you to get a dog, Nixie. You know I do."

"*I* meant it," Lucy said.

Maybe *she'd* turn out to be a dog person.

Maybe she'd turn out to be an amazing dog person. Maybe dogs would be her special thing, the way they were Nixie's. It would be all right to have the same special thing as someone else so long as you weren't in the same family, she decided—the same way Nolan and Elena both had coding as their special thing.

She could already see a dog-walking badge taped onto her Let's Have Fun Club sash.

★ six ★

It rained that weekend, so it wasn't dog-walking weather. Lucy had a feeling even Nixie wouldn't find it fun to pick up extra-large dog poop in the rain.

But a rainy Saturday was perfect weather for coding.

First Elena had her hour of computer time and then she lay on the family room couch lost in a book.

So, boldly, Lucy sat down at the computer, set the timer for her own hour, called up the same computer website they used at camp, and clicked on the maze program. It was thrilling to send her boat sailing along merrily through even harder mazes, all by herself, without Preston or Pippa, without Nolan—just Lucy.

Half an hour later, Lucy heard Elena set

her book down on the coffee table. She turned around to see Elena staring her way.

"What are *you* doing?" Elena asked, in an accusing tone.

What did Elena think she was doing?

"Coding," Lucy said, as if she did coding all the time, as if she had just as much right to use the computer as Elena did—and didn't she?

"Great!" Elena snapped. "You and I only have *one* computer for homework *and* coding and *everything*. So now I'm going to have to wait around all the time for my turn until *your* turn is done?"

Well, Lucy had been the one who had done all the waiting around so far.

"You already had your hour," Lucy made herself say.

"But now I need the computer for homework," Elena shot back.

Lucy looked at the timer. "I'll be done in twenty-eight minutes." Though she had just used up two minutes arguing with Elena.

Elena snatched up her book and stomped upstairs. Lucy could hear the door of their bedroom slam behind her.

There were still twenty-seven minutes and thirteen seconds left on the timer. But it was hard to steer a boat through a maze when the sound of the slammed door was ringing in Lucy's ears.

★ ★ ★

Week two of coding camp began with a presentation from a guest speaker who used coding to make special light and sound effects for a local dance company. She looked exactly the way Lucy expected a dancer to look: tall and slim, with her hair pulled back tightly from her face in a non-messy bun. The video she showed was amazing. Lucy hadn't known coding could be used for real-life dances by human beings, not just animated dances by cartoon creatures.

After the presentation, Preston said this would be the week for dance choreography. *Choreography* meant telling dancers the sequence of steps and movements to perform.

This would be the week Lucy learned how to make her own dances for her own hipping-hopping kangaroo!

"Let's code a dance right now, in our room,"

Pippa said. She and Preston liked what they called "unplugged" activities, where you learned about coding without even using a computer. Lucy thought those activities were fun, too.

Pippa turned on some music with a catchy beat, at a volume low enough that she could speak over it.

"First, let's make a list of possible moves to include in our dance."

What would count as a dance move? Lucy tried to remember what steps Elena's kangaroo and hedgehog had done, but she didn't know the names of any of them.

The other kids seemed baffled, too, even Nolan. So Pippa demonstrated a few: a clap high, a dab, a floss, and a funny one called Gangnam.

"Now let's put them in an algorithm," Pippa said. "Let's decide which *order* to do them in — and how *long* to do each one. Two measures? Four measures? Six?"

Pippa counted out the beats of the music. "*One*, two, three, four. *One*, two, three, four. *One*, two, three, four." She explained that each "one two three four" was a measure, and that she'd just counted out three measures.

After ten more minutes of demonstration, Pippa had the sequence of dance motions written on the classroom Smart Board with the number of measures, chosen by the campers, next to each one.

"And we'll just keep on following this choreography code, in a loop, till the music ends. Get it?" Pippa asked.

Everyone nodded.

Pippa cranked up the volume on the music. "So now let's dance it!"

Lucy tried doing the dance, following Pippa's example, but the movements changed too quickly. *One*, two, three, four; *one*, two, three, four; *one*, two, three, four; *one*, two, three, four went by so fast when you were trying to do a clap high while it happened. Dancing clearly wasn't going to turn out to be her best thing. It was more fun just to watch everyone else.

Nolan was good at remembering the motions for each dance move. But the serious expression on his face was such a contrast to

the silliness of the motions, it made Lucy want to laugh.

Vera worked so hard to get every step perfect that she was still trying to do the dab when the rest of the campers were on to the floss.

Nixie looked pleased with herself even when she got the motions wrong. She gave huge smiles to an imaginary audience as if she were dancing in a show on Broadway.

As Boogie tried to keep up with the music's pulsing beat, he flung out his arm for the double-down so energetically he narrowly missed smacking Vera in the face.

"Sorry!" he panted.

Then when he tried to do the Gangnam move, he stumbled against the side of a desk.

"Ow!" He stopped to rub his hip.

The song finally came to a stop, and Pippa clicked off the music.

"Well?" she said. "What did you think of our dance?"

"Dancing is hard!" one kid from another group moaned. Lucy certainly agreed.

"What made it hard?" Pippa asked him.

"Um—everything?"

"The desk crashed into me!" Boogie said, and got a big laugh, but not from Vera.

"So," Pippa said, "one thing that made it hard was not having enough space to do your motions, so you bumped into each other and the furniture. What else made it hard?"

"It all went too fast," someone in the front of the room said.

"So . . . maybe the dance moves should change after six or eight measures, not two or four," Pippa suggested. "Anything else?"

"It's too hot in here!" came another complaint.

Pippa smiled. "Well, that's something we won't have to worry about in our computer-coded choreography. Our animated dancers don't sweat! But once we start coding for *several* animated dancers, we'll have to watch for how we position them on the screen so they aren't so close they'll bump into each other. And we'll have to make a sequence of the steps so the dance isn't too frenetic and jerky—unless that's the look you want, of course. It's up to you."

"And don't let Boogie be one of the dancers!"

Nixie joked, but not loud enough for Pippa and Preston to hear.

Boogie made a low bow, as if she had complimented him, and then caught himself just before he toppled over. Vera didn't smile this time, either.

Boogie and Vera were just so different, Lucy thought. Boogie's thing was goofing off and being silly; Vera's thing was working hard and being serious. And right now it didn't seem like coding was Vera's thing *or* Boogie's thing. But Boogie didn't seem to mind if something wasn't his thing, and Vera did—even if she already had *two* other things, comics *and* piano.

Right now Lucy still didn't have anything to be *her* thing at all.

★ ★ ★

Coding a dance was even more fun than coding a boat in a maze. There were so many choices to make: picking the dancer, the music, the moves, even special background effects. And that was just for a dance with one dancer. When you added more dancers, they could be side by side, or in a square or in a circle. They could be the same size or different sizes, so that one was the main dancer in front, and the others danced behind her. They could be doing the same motions in unison, or each dancer could be doing a different motion. It depended on what instructions you put in the code.

Lucy chose a duck, to have something different from Elena's kangaroo, and the disco song her dad liked to play when he washed the car, and a disco-ball background with bursts of bright light.

Yay for a disco-dancing duck!

Nolan already had his giraffe flanked by two smaller monkey backup dancers. Nixie had chosen a dog as her dancer—surprise, surprise—but was still trying to decide which music a dog would like best.

Vera would code one movement for one measure for her dancing mouse, and then run the program to see how it looked. Then she'd add another motion for another measure, and run the program to see how *it* looked. At the rate she was going, it would take her a whole month to get through one single mouse dance.

Boogie's hippo was as clumsy a dancer as

Boogie had been. His hippo was dancing right on top of his dancing turtle.

"Ouch!" Boogie said, on behalf of his turtle. "Get off me, you great big hippo!"

Lucy laughed, and this time Vera laughed with her. It was hard not to laugh with Boogie.

But Lucy was glad her duck was such a good dancer.

"I know you're saving each program you code," Preston said. "But now is a good time for a reminder to keep on doing this. Our last day of camp is going to be our Coding Expo, when your family and friends can come see the amazing things you've coded during our time together. They're going to want to see some of these dances, for sure!"

Lucy remembered she hadn't gone to the Coding Expo for Elena's coding camp because she had been home sick with a bad cold that day.

Would Elena come to hers?

If she did, what would she think of Lucy's dancing duck?

Would she be mad that Lucy's duck danced just as well as Elena's kangaroo?

What if her duck danced . . . even better?

★ seven ★

By the end of the week, Lucy thought her dancers were definitely good enough to earn a dancing badge. Well, a computer-dancing badge. She was still impressed at how exhausting real dancing had been.

It had been hard to get her hour of computer time at home each day. Elena kept claiming she needed the computer for "homework" and then quickly turning off the monitor if anyone walked by. When Lucy did get her turn, Elena stalked out of the room, except for one time when she had seen Lucy working on a dance sequence. Then she stood behind the computer and made comments like, *Those two dancers are too close together* and *Those dance steps don't fit with that music.*

If only human beings could be more like dancing animals in a coding program! The computer's dancing animals did exactly what you told them to do every single time, even if by mistake you told them to do something ridiculous, like dance on top of someone else's head. But it was impossible to make other people—especially older sisters—do what you wanted them to do.

Lucy wished she could write a computer code like this:

1. If Lucy sits down at the computer, then Elena smiles.

2. If Lucy is coding a dance, then Elena says, *Good job!*

3. If Lucy finishes her hour, then Elena says, *Should we start planning out what we need to do for our coding badge?*

Lucy hadn't mentioned the badge to Elena since the day she had asked their mom to sign her up for coding camp. She was afraid that if she did, Elena might just stomp away and slam the bedroom door again.

★ ★ ★

Saturday was the day Lucy and Nixie had arranged to meet at Boogie's house at two o'clock to walk Boogie's dog.

That morning, sitting cross-legged on her bed, Lucy started writing down the requirements for a dog-walking badge in the Let's Have Fun Club handbook.

Elena looked over her shoulder.

"A *dog*-walking badge?" she asked. "We don't *have* a dog." It was the same thing Nolan had pointed out to Nixie.

"I'm borrowing a dog," Lucy told her. "Well, me and someone else."

She read Elena the list of possible items for the badge, including the things she had made up in her head the other day: walk a dog, pick up dog poop, go running with a dog, play fetch with a dog, and take a dog to a dog park.

Elena shook her head. "We should have to walk at least two different dogs. Probably three. Of different sizes and breeds. Or walk two dogs at the same time. Or have someone pay us to walk a dog."

How could *Elena*, who had never walked a dog in her life, be making up requirements for *Lucy*'s dog-walking badge? But the way Elena had said *we* and *us* gave Lucy a little tingle of happiness. Maybe Elena would want to get a dog-walking badge, too! Maybe Elena was going to start caring about the Let's Have Fun Club again.

Would now be a good time to mention the coding badge?

But, relieved to see Elena's interest in the dog-walking requirements, Lucy just said, "Ooh! Those are amazing ideas!" She added them to the list in the handbook.

But today she just needed to walk one dog. And pick up the poop of one dog. And find out if she might be a dog person like Nixie, if loving dogs might be *her* special thing.

★ ★ ★

Boogie lived just a few blocks away, so Lucy walked there. Just as her parents believed in old-fashioned activities for kids, they also believed in old-fashioned transportation.

When Lucy turned the corner onto Boogie's street, she spotted Nixie and Boogie already outside in Boogie's well-trampled front yard with the biggest dog Lucy had ever seen. From a distance he looked more like a bear than a dog.

"This is Bear!" Nixie shouted joyfully. "We're going to walk him to the park!"

So the bear-size dog was even named Bear.

"He's all yours," Boogie said, as he handed Bear's leash to Nixie. "Oh, and the poop bags are in the pouch hanging from the leash," Boogie called after them before he disappeared into the house.

As Lucy approached, Bear dashed up to her, dragging Nixie along behind him. The next thing Lucy knew, Bear's huge wet tongue was licking as many parts of Lucy as he could reach.

"Sit, Bear!" Nixie commanded, as if she had bossed around hundreds of dogs before.

Bear didn't listen.

"Sit, Bear!" Nixie said, louder this time, and she yanked at his leash.

This time Bear dropped down onto the

lawn, grinning up at Lucy with his huge wet tongue hanging out of his huge toothy mouth.

"Do you think he bites?" Lucy had to ask.

"No. He's a Saint Bernard. You know, the ones who rescue people from avalanches in Switzerland? The ones who carry those little thermoses of hot chocolate around their necks so the rescued people won't freeze to death? A dog like that wouldn't bite people."

Lucy hoped Nixie was right.

As Lucy stayed a safe distance behind, Nixie started down the sidewalk.

Bear stopped to pee four times in the first block.

"Ewww!" Lucy said before she could stop herself.

"Good boy!" Nixie praised Bear, as if peeing were a spectacular accomplishment.

Then, just before they reached the corner, Bear squatted to make a poop.

Lucy was too horrified to say anything this time. Boogie hadn't been joking about the need for extra-big poop bags.

"Good dog!" Nixie praised him again, but even Nixie had turned a bit pale.

Feeling like a traitor, Lucy squinched her eyes shut as Nixie dealt with scooping up what needed to be scooped. Maybe it wasn't too late to change the dog-walking-badge rules to leave out anything having to do with dog poop.

But she wouldn't be able to give herself any credit toward the badge today if she didn't at least hold Bear's leash for a little while.

"Can I hold the leash now?" she asked Nixie, once the poop bag had been deposited in the trash can at the entrance to the park.

"Okay," Nixie said reluctantly. "But you have to hold it *tight*. Bear is *big*."

As if Lucy hadn't already noticed.

At first Bear trotted along beside Lucy obediently. Then Bear saw another dog, a tiny fluff ball hardly bigger than Bear's head, entering the park with his middle-aged owner.

At the sight of Bear, the man's face lit up with recognition. "Bear!" he greeted Boogie's dog. "What lovely young ladies are walking you today?"

At the sound of his name, Bear made an enormous leap toward the man and the little dog. The next thing Lucy knew, she was facedown on the gravel path as Bear and his leash dashed off for a sniffing frenzy with the fluff-ball dog.

"Are you all right?" the man asked Lucy as he helped her up. "Gosh, I'm sorry."

"I guess so," Lucy managed to say. Her knees were scraped, but not bleeding. She brushed gravel off her chin and from her hair.

Now Lucy knew: she was definitely not a dog person.

Dogs were definitely not her thing.

"You really truly *liked* walking Bear?" she asked Nixie, once Bear had been returned to Boogie.

Nixie stared at her. "Of course! Okay, I can see why you didn't like it today. Bear is pretty big for a starter dog. You'd *adore* dogs if you had a smaller one first. My *parents* would adore dogs if they'd only let me get one. Do you have any brothers or sisters?"

Lucy was puzzled by the question. "I have a sister. Older than me."

"You're lucky! I'm an only child, so it's just

me against my parents. If *I* had a sister, we'd beg *together* for a dog, and we'd *make* them give in."

Lucy thought about this for a moment. She and Elena had never made their parents give in about anything. Well, Elena had made them let her do coding camp, and then they had let Lucy do it, too. But the two of them hadn't done their begging *together*. Elena hadn't even wanted Lucy to do the coding camp at all.

Lucy had to ask the next question. "What if your sister liked dogs first, and wanted to be the only one who liked them? Would you have to like cats then?"

Nixie stared at her even longer and harder this time.

"Of course not! If I had a sister, which I don't, we'd both love dogs; and if I had a dog, which I don't, he'd love both of us. That's just how it is with dogs—and how it is with sisters."

Nixie certainly sounded sure of herself for someone who didn't have either a dog *or* a sister.

★ eight ★

"All right, coders," Preston said on Monday afternoon, the first day of the third week of camp.

"Last week you were dancers and choreographers. This week you're going to be artists and animators. Actually, you've been animators all along. Animators just create an algorithm by putting images in order, one after the other, to make an object look as if it's moving—a boat in a maze, a dancer, even letters of the alphabet."

He showed a short video on how to take letters—like the letters of your name—and make them change color, twirl around, jump up and down, and even make sounds.

The videos always made everything look so easy. Lucy already knew real coding was hard. (Elena had been right about that.) Every single thing every single letter did had to be put into code. There was no code instruction for telling a letter, *Jump!* the way Preston had told Nixie, *Walk!* You had to tell the letter to move up so many spaces, and then move down so many spaces, and how fast to do it. You couldn't just tell a letter, *Now turn pink!* You had to choose the exact shade of color on a spectrum and the brightness of the color— everything.

It was a good thing Lucy liked coding!

"This sounds impossible," Vera said sadly, once the video had finished.

"You'll be great at it!" Nixie reassured Vera. Lucy remembered Nixie had said Vera drew amazing comics. "Now you'll be able to make animated comics! You can turn your comics into movies! You'll win the Academy Award for best animated film, and Nolan, Lucy, Boogie, and I will come to the Oscars and you can thank us in your speech!"

Vera shook her head at Nixie's enthusiasm, but she was smiling.

First Preston showed them how to use a little paintbrush icon on the computer to draw images using the computer touchpad to move the brush along.

Sure enough, Vera was good at drawing with the strange new paintbrush. She drew a dog that looked just like a dog.

Lucy tried to copy Vera's picture. But what she really wanted was to start coding her dog to move around the screen.

Nixie tried to draw a dog, too, of course, but Vera's had turned out so much better than hers that she just admired Vera's dog instead.

The cat Nolan drew wasn't as good as Vera's dog. So drawing wasn't Nolan's thing. It was a relief that there was something in the world Nolan wasn't best at.

Boogie clearly drew a terrible dog on purpose. His dog was a blob with four lines coming down from the blob to be legs, and another smaller blob stuck on top of the bigger blob to be a head.

When it came time for their animals to move, Lucy learned they weren't going to make them actually move their arms and legs. They were just going to make the little picture of the animal, as a unit, move around the screen. But that was hard enough.

Lucy felt giddy when she managed to make her dog move first to the left, then to the right, then up, and then down. It felt miraculous that little blocks of code clicked into place could make something happen on the screen exactly the way you wanted it to.

"Cool!" Nolan said, looking over at her screen. And when Lucy looked over at his, she saw her dog was moving every bit as well as his cat.

Now that the drawing part was done and the coding part had begun, Vera had turned back to being as fidgety and flustered as she always was when she had to code anything.

"My dog won't jump!" Vera moaned. "He just sits there like a lump!"

"Blobby sits there like a lump, too," Boogie said cheerfully. He had named his blob dog Blobby. "His full name is Blobby Q. Lumpy."

"What does *Q* stand for?" Nixie asked.

Boogie thought for a moment. "It doesn't stand for anything."

Vera gave a little moan of annoyance.

"Nolan?" Nixie called over to him. "What's Vera doing wrong?"

Vera never asked anyone for help; Lucy could tell Vera hated to be a bother. Nixie was always the one who did the asking for her. Nixie was so good at pestering people, it was amazing she hadn't yet managed to pester her parents into getting her a dog, even if she didn't have a sibling to pester with her.

But Nolan was busy rescuing someone else in another group. He was practically an assistant teacher for the camp, helping almost as many kids as Preston and Pippa did.

Vera answered the question for her: "Everything! I'm doing everything wrong!"

But Lucy knew that wasn't the right answer. Nobody ever did everything wrong with their coding. Well, maybe except Boogie. There had to be one particular bit of the code that was incorrect. All you had to do was find it and fix it.

Lucy peered at Vera's screen.

Vera had told the dog to start jumping when she clicked on a little green flag at the top of the screen, but then Vera had kept clicking the space bar over and over again. Clicking the space bar was another possible "event" for starting a program, but that wasn't the way Vera had coded it.

"Try this," Lucy said. She clicked on the green flag. Instantly Vera's dog started bouncing.

"Yay!" Nixie, Vera, and Boogie said together.

"Lucy is a genius!" Nixie squealed. "Lucy is the most genius-y of all geniuses!"

Lucy felt herself blushing. What she had done was so simple! It didn't take a genius— let alone the most genius-y of all geniuses—to notice one simple error and correct it.

But still. She had done it.

Not Nolan.

Not Elena.

Lucy.

She was the most genius-y of all geniuses in her coding group at coding camp today.

Maybe that should be an item on Lucy's

coding badge, if she ever made up the rules for one: solve a coding problem for someone else.

And she had already done it!

Nolan was back now. "What do you need help with?" he asked Vera.

"Lucy already fixed it!" Nixie reported.

Would Nolan look cross that he wasn't the only code-fixer-person in their group now? Would he tell Lucy that coding was *his* thing, so it couldn't be hers?

Instead, his face crinkled into a huge grin as he raised his hand to give her a high five.

Lucy's face hurt from grinning as she high-fived him back.

★ ★ ★

By Friday they were supposed to be completing the code for animating the letters of their name, or at least their initials. Not that Pippa and Preston ever gave deadlines or nagged anybody to hurry up and finish any coding task. They kept saying that play was the best way to learn coding. They thought play was the best way to learn anything.

Vera's letters still weren't cooperating. *V*, *E*, and *R* were doing what they were supposed to,

but her *A* bounced so high it disappeared off the top of the screen.

"Nolan? Lucy?" Nixie said. "Can you guys make Vera's *A* behave?"

Nolan started to get up from his seat to stand behind Vera's computer.

Then he sat back down again.

"I just need to fix this one thing in my own code," he said. But Lucy had a feeling Nolan's code was already working perfectly. Nolan's own code always worked perfectly.

Should she go help Vera and be the most genius-y of all geniuses again? But something about the way Nolan had stopped himself from helping made Lucy want to see what would happen if no one came to rescue Vera.

Boogie looked over at Vera's computer. As if Boogie could help anybody fix anything!

"I like the flowers you added to your letters," he said. "They look like they're growing out of them. Maybe I should add something onto Blobby."

Even though everyone else had been busy with the name-animation challenge for the last three days, Boogie was content to make

Blobby twitch occasionally or roll over once in a while. "Like ears!" Boogie said. "Maybe Blobby would listen better if I gave him some ears! That would help, I know it—"

Vera cut Boogie off with a wail. "I just touched something that made my *A* come back again, and then you started talking, talking, talking, about Blobby, Blobby, Blobby, and I got distracted, and I hit the wrong key somehow, and now my *A* is gone again!"

Lucy had never heard Vera sound angry before. Even when Boogie had almost whacked her in the face during the real-life dance chore-ography, she had barely given him a scowl.

"Just because *you* don't care about doing anything right doesn't mean *I* don't care. My *A* with the yellow daisies on it, the one I had to draw three times to get it right, is *gone*! It's gone, and I can't get it *back*!"

She didn't add, *And it's your fault!* but Lucy knew that was what she was thinking.

Pippa called over to Vera. "Hold on, Preston or I will be there in a minute." To the whole class, she said, "Everybody, listen: I'm hearing too many people freaking out right now. Just remember: If what you're doing isn't working, *try something else.* Remember, this is Computer *Play* Camp!"

"I'm sorry," Boogie said, in a small, un-Boogie-like voice.

"Just look at it!" Vera cried, pointing to her screen. Lucy could see Vera's *A* was still missing.

Obediently, Boogie looked where Vera was pointing. He stared at the screen as if staring could cause a vanished *A* to reappear.

"One time . . ." Boogie said, and trailed off. "One time I was messing around with Blobby—okay, I know you're tired of hearing about Blobby—but Blobby disappeared, and then I touched this one thing, and he came back."

As Lucy held her breath, Boogie leaned over and touched something on Vera's computer for her.

There was *A*! Wreathed with daisies, and at the end of Vera's name, exactly where it was supposed to be!

For a moment no one said anything.

Then Nixie said, "It's fixed!"

In a choked voice, Vera said, "Boogie fixed it."

"Boogie fixed it!" Nolan sounded as proud of Boogie as Boogie always was of Nolan.

"Well, Blobby helped," Boogie said modestly.

Vera just stared at her screen. "But—but—but all you do is goof off!" she told Boogie. "I'm trying so hard, and you're not trying at all, so how could *you* fix *my* dog?"

Boogie shrugged. "Luck?"

Lucy had an idea. She wasn't sure she should say it. But so often in coding camp, she would have an idea and *not* say it, and then Nolan *would* say it, and it would solve everything.

"Maybe . . ." she said to Vera. "Maybe you're trying *too* hard? And maybe Boogie isn't trying hard enough?" She remembered what Pippa had just said. "I mean, if what you're doing isn't working, maybe you should try—"

"Something else," Vera and Boogie said together.

Lucy continued. "Like maybe Vera should just try—"

"Playing?" Vera asked with a sigh. She

made it sound as if playing was the hardest work anyone had ever had to do.

Fifteen minutes later, Vera had somehow managed to get her *A* to cooperate with *V*, *E*, and *R*.

"I just tried a bunch of things," she said, "and then one of them worked!"

And in those fifteen minutes, Boogie had managed to make Blobby do a clumsy little bouncing dance.

"Look at Blobby!" Boogie shouted. "Did you ever see a blob dance like that? Look at him go!"

Lucy sat admiring her own animated name on the screen, *L-U-C-Y*, with each letter doing its own carefully choreographed motions, one after the other, in perfect sequence.

Maybe . . . *could* coding possibly be *her* thing, after all?

★ nine ★

On Sunday afternoon, while Elena was off at Juniper's house, Lucy lay on the couch, finally starting to write down the requirements for a Let's Have Fun Club coding badge. Maybe when Elena saw them written officially in the handbook, she'd get excited the way she had started to get excited about the dog-walking badge.

Lucy put the handbook down on the coffee table after she had a list of half a dozen items, and then set the timer for her computer hour. It was bliss to be able to use her computer time in perfect freedom. She wanted to try out some new ideas for animating her name. It would be cool to start with all the letters doing the same thing, and then have them change, one letter at a time. What if her *L* turned a somersault, and then her *U* jumped up and down, and her *C* jiggled like Jell-O, and her *Y* bounced right off the screen and then right back onto it again?

This would be the best animated name in the history of the world!

She giggled, thinking how much she sounded like Nixie now.

But when her name was done, it was amazing to watch the letters doing amazing things that *she*, Lucy Lopez, had told them to do.

She sensed someone behind her and whirled around to see Elena, clutching the Let's Have Fun Club handbook as if she might hurl it at the computer screen.

"I thought you were at Juniper's," Lucy said, realizing too late how guilty it made her sound. But she didn't have to feel guilty for using her own hour of computer time—she didn't!

"Well, I'm not," Elena said. "For your information, Juniper threw up. Twice. So Dad came to get me. For obvious reasons."

With a shaking finger she pointed to the open page of the handbook.

"So *you're* the one making up requirements for a coding badge, when you wanted to do coding only because *I* did it first? And now you're the big know-it-all about coding? *Number four: Animate the letters of your name in three different ways.* We didn't even do that activity in my camp. *Number five: Help someone else with a coding problem.* So now *you're* the great coder guru, helping everyone else with their coding problems? What makes you think I'd even want to get another stupid fake badge from a stupid fake club—especially a stupid fake badge *you'd* get only because you copied *me*?"

Lucy felt her cheeks flushing, not with guilt, but with anger of her own to match Elena's.

"Why *shouldn't* we both get a coding badge? We both got the bracelet-making badge. We both got the reading badge. We both got the jigsaw-puzzle badge. We both got the hair badge. We're both working together on the cookie-baking badge."

"That's right," Elena snapped. "Why don't you get a badge for doing *every single thing*

I do? You already copy everything else about me. I picked out those running shoes with the light-up sparkles, and then you asked Mom for the very same ones."

But half the girls in Lucy's class had those light-up sparkle shoes!

"I did my third-grade life-cycle-of-an-animal report on porcupines, and then last month you did your life-cycle report on porcupines, too!"

How was Lucy supposed to remember what animal Elena had chosen for her animal report two *years* ago?

"And then you went to Mom behind my back to get her to sign you up for coding camp. You couldn't let there be *one* thing that's all mine, could you? Not one thing in the whole entire *universe*!"

Elena ended with a sound that was half gulp, half sob. And then Lucy couldn't feel angry anymore.

Oh, why *had* she ever signed up for coding camp? Why *hadn't* she let Elena have one thing in the universe that was all hers? She could still quit the camp. She would quit the camp tomorrow. All the fun she'd had with coding for the last three weeks wasn't worth making her sister feel so miserable. She didn't want coding to be her thing if it was going to make tears start running down Elena's cheeks.

If only she had turned out to have a talent for basketball, like Nolan. If only she liked dogs as much as Nixie did. Although she might have liked dogs better if Bear hadn't been so big and so . . . doggy. Maybe walking smaller, better-behaved dogs could be her one special thing.

Or maybe she'd never have one thing in the universe that was all hers, either.

"I'm sorry," Lucy whispered, with a half gulp, half sob of her own.

Through a veil of tears, she stumbled into the hall and ran upstairs. Alone in their room, she found her Let's Have Fun Club sash, tucked carefully in a safe corner of her upper bureau drawer. It felt good to rip off all four badges. Then she started into the sash—tearing, tearing, tearing.

Tiny scraps of crepe paper rained down on the bedroom carpet like confetti.

★ ★ ★

Elena must have thrown away the scraps from Lucy's torn-up sash because they were gone when Lucy came to bed that night, after a dinner where both girls hardly said a word. Lucy was glad to have the room to herself while Elena was still downstairs watching TV.

She lay in bed hugging her pillow, trying to forget how terrible it had been to hear Elena's sobs and to see Elena's tears.

If only, once Lucy quit coding camp, everything would go back to the way it used to be.

★ ★ ★

Lucy waited until the next morning to tell her parents she didn't want to go to coding camp anymore. Even though her dad had seemed willing to let her quit on that first day, three weeks ago, she had a feeling they'd be upset if she quit now, with only one week left to go. Both her parents believed in *sticking things out*. They were both big on *following through*. And if they asked why she suddenly wanted to quit, and she told them the truth, they might be mad at Elena, and then Elena would be even madder and sadder than she was already.

But Lucy didn't have to tell them the truth. She could just say she had finally figured out she wasn't a coding person, the way Vera had calmly announced she wasn't a dog person. Some people weren't coding people, just like some people weren't dog people—even if Nixie thought everyone in the world should be a dog person, even her own nonexistent sister.

"Dad?" she asked after breakfast, once Elena had left to brush her teeth. "I've been thinking, and . . ."

She could tell her father was too busy fixing lunches to be listening, so she let her sentence trail off.

Would Nixie still like dogs even if she had a sister who liked dogs first? It was hard to imagine Nixie switching to loving cats instead.

"And *what*, honey?" her dad asked. He had been listening, after all. "What have you been thinking?"

Lucy shook her head. "Nothing."

"Nothing?" her father gently pursued. "You

girls were both so quiet at dinner last night. Is something wrong between you?"

Everything was wrong between them!

But Nixie truly seemed to think it was perfectly fine for two people in the same family to like the same thing. If Nixie had a sister who loved dogs, Nixie would love dogs, anyway. Nixie would never give up on loving what she loved.

"No," Lucy said to her dad. "I wasn't thinking anything."

Except that maybe, just maybe, Nixie was right.

★ ten ★

For the final week of camp, Pippa told them on Monday afternoon, they'd be learning how to take the first steps toward coding their own simple computer games.

The camp erupted into pandemonium. Two boys at the front of the room gave a good imitation of missiles blasting. Another boy fell off his chair onto the floor, clutching his chest as if he were dead.

Lucy saw Colleen catch Pippa's eye and give a warning shake of her head.

"These will not be violent games," Pippa hastened to add.

The missile-exploders and fake dead boy groaned in disappointment.

Lucy hadn't played many computer games. Her parents liked old-fashioned board games or games played in what they called *the great outdoors*. But she couldn't wait to learn how to code one.

Pippa explained that every game had to have an *objective*—a goal the players were trying to accomplish. Otherwise you'd never know whether you had won. Games had to have *rules* for what the players were allowed to do to reach the goal. Games were more challenging when players had to overcome *obstacles* along the way.

The first game they were learning to code was an easy one, where a little ball had to jump through a gap between two moving posts.

Lucy worked half-heartedly on coding the moving-ball game. It was hard to care about a little bouncing ball on the screen when your real-life sister wasn't speaking to you, and you didn't know how you were ever going to make things right between the two of you ever again.

"My ball *wants* to hit the posts," Boogie said, but then he gave a sheepish grin. "But I bet he could get through them if he wanted to. And if I figured out how to help him."

He stared at his screen, forehead furrowed.

"Come on, ball!" Boogie encouraged the screen. "Come on, Ballie! Come on, little Ballie-Wallie!"

Then Boogie gave a shout. "Ballie did it! I mean, *I* did it! Okay, Ballie, I'm going to change the game to make it harder for you. I'm going to make the gap between the posts smaller. Are you ready, Ballie?"

"Sure!" he made Ballie squeak.

Vera had been giving her own little squeaks of agitation as she tried to figure out how the game was supposed to operate.

"My ball wants to hit the posts, too," she confessed to Boogie. "I don't know how to fix the game so he can get through."

"Your Ballie just needs to mess around for a while, to build up his confidence," Boogie suggested. "Like this." He leaned over Vera's computer. The next thing Lucy knew, Vera was giggling. Her Ballie might still be crashing into the posts, but at least he was having fun. And it looked like Vera was having fun, too.

But Lucy wasn't having fun. All she could think about was Elena's words: *You couldn't let there be* one *thing that's all mine, could you? Not one thing in the whole entire* universe!

Elena didn't even seem like a sister right now, more like an alien who had showed up at the house from a faraway galaxy to share a bedroom with her. Talking to Elena—if she ever did talk to Elena again—would be like talking to those aliens from the first day of coding camp.

How *would* she talk to Elena if Elena was really an alien? She'd have to spell out everything super-clearly.

It's all right for two sisters to like the same thing!

But maybe an alien wouldn't know what a *sister* was.

Lucy remembered how Nixie had tried to explain *pets* to an alien. She had said a pet was a special kind of animal who loves you better than anyone in the world.

A sister, Lucy could say, is a special kind of human being who loves you better than anyone in the world.

It suddenly occurred to Lucy that no one, not even Nolan, had pointed out to Nixie that she'd also need to explain *love* to the alien.

How could you ever explain love to an alien? Or to a computer?

Or to a sister?

★ ★ ★

The next three camp days were devoted to making their own computer games. Friday, the last day of camp, would be the Coding Expo, where the campers could show off their dances, their animated names, their games— everything!

But it was as hard for Lucy to focus on making her own game as it had been to focus on Monday's sample game. So on Tuesday she just watched what everyone else was making. Maybe she *should* have quit coding camp if she wasn't going to be doing any coding anymore.

Nolan's game, which he had started working on at home, was already so complex no one understood it when he explained it to them, not even Lucy. But from what she could hear, it had plenty of explosive sound effects.

"But no people, animals, or property are harmed in the playing of the game," Nolan assured them.

Nixie's game was exactly like the bouncing-ball game, only with a bouncing dog instead of a bouncing ball. Every time the dog bounced through the posts, you got a point. If you got ten points, your parents had to get you a dog. Nixie's parents couldn't come to the expo because of work, but she planned to play her game with them on the computer at home.

"They're terrible at games," Nixie gloated. "And I'm the one who made the game, so I'm bound to be good at it, so I'll win, and I'll get a dog! And I'll get one you'll love to walk, Lucy! And you too, Vera!"

To Lucy's astonishment, Vera and Boogie decided to make their game together. Well, she would have been astonished a week ago, but she wasn't astonished now. The game had Blobby in it, and Vera drew a face on him with a jolly expression just like Boogie's. The objective of the game was for Blobby to wander around at random until he bumped into a big green dot, and then the dot turned into a flower.

"Do you get a point for every dot that turns into a flower?" Nolan asked.

Vera and Boogie both shook their heads.

"So what *do* you get?"

"You get pretty flowers," Vera said.

"Vera's drawing the flowers," Boogie added. "So they'll be *very* pretty flowers."

And just like that, Lucy had an idea—a wonderful idea, an absolutely perfect idea—for her game.

If only Elena would come to the expo! And if only Elena would play Lucy's game!

★ ★ ★

The Coding Expo was held in their classroom, but Colleen had gotten permission for it to spill out into the hallway, to have enough space for fifteen coders and their guests.

Lucy hadn't mentioned the expo to Elena, and Elena hadn't mentioned it to Lucy. They tried to act normal in front of their parents, but when it was just the two of them, they had barely talked about anything since their big fight on Sunday.

As Lucy sat with her open computer, at a desk in the hall near the library, she waited to see when her parents would come, and if Elena would be with them.

Would Elena criticize her choreographed

dances? Get mad that Lucy knew how to animate letters when Elena hadn't done that in her camp? Most important, would she refuse to play the game?

Next to Lucy, Boogie sat showing Colleen how he had coded the moves for one of Blobby's dance routines. Vera, Nixie, and Nolan had their desks next in the row. Their families weren't there yet, either.

"Wow!" Colleen said. "This is so cool!" She lowered her voice. "Believe it or not, I'm terrible at computers. But you're a good teacher, Boogie. I think I could code a dance for my own Blobby now, if you helped me."

Boogie beamed. Lucy felt herself beaming, too. Yay for Blobby, and yay for Boogie!

Then she looked up, and there was Elena.

"Mom and Dad are coming later," Elena said stiffly. "They said I should come over to your expo now, without them, because they had to 'finish up a couple of things' first. And you know what *that* means."

Nervous as she felt, Lucy stifled a giggle. Their parents were always *finishing up a couple of things* in their classrooms, and their *couple of things* always took forever.

Elena giggled, too, and suddenly both girls were laughing hysterically in their old hyena way. It was so good to laugh together again! It was the best thing in the world!

A moment later, the laughter ended abruptly, as if the laughing sound effect on a computer game had been shut off.

It was time for Lucy to ask the question that mattered to her most. "Do you want to play the game I made?"

Elena avoided Lucy's eyes. "What's it called?"

Lucy took a deep breath. "It's called *Sisters*."

Elena opened her mouth as if she was about to say something. But then she closed it as if she had changed her mind about saying anything.

Lucy handed her the set of instructions she had typed up and printed out.

The objective of this game is to gather a bunch of flowers to give your sister.

Elena still didn't say anything, but Lucy could see her eyes glistening.

Like Vera and Boogie's game, Lucy's game involved flowers, but hers was more of a real game than theirs, because you had to figure out how to catch flowers that were floating through the air and put them into a vase. When you got ten flowers, a girl appeared on the screen, with long dark hair, like Elena. Lucy had been so glad when she found that figure in the program's catalog of ready-made pictures you could put into the code. Even Vera couldn't have drawn one as good.

"Go on, play it," Lucy begged.

When Elena looked up from the end-of-game screen with its bunch of flowers for the girl who looked like her, she wiped her eyes with the side of her hand.

"I made something for you, too," she said, sounding as shy as Lucy had.

From her backpack, she pulled out a brand-new Let's Have Fun Club sash with four badges on it, exactly like the one Lucy had ripped into a hundred tiny pieces.

"I'm sorry I was mean," Elena said. "I guess we can't help liking so many of the same things. It sort of makes sense, because we're—"

"Sisters," Lucy finished the sentence for her.

"And I started making a new badge," Elena continued. "Wait till you see this. You aren't going to believe it."

She reached into her backpack for the Let's Have Fun Club handbook and gave it to Lucy.

Lucy flipped past the dog-walking badge and the coding badge, to a page that read:

SISTERS BADGE

1. Do the dishes for your sister some night even if it's her turn, just to be nice.

2. Stick up for your sister if someone else is mean to her.

3. If you do anything mean yourself, tell your sister you're sorry.

4. Help your sister get a badge.

5. Give your sister a great big hug.

"I love this badge," Lucy whispered. "It's my favorite badge of all."

"And I just did number three on the list," Elena crowed. "And I helped you with the hair badge, so that's number four for me. And if you show me how to do the name-animation thing for the coding badge, then that's number four for you, too."

"Let's cross off number five right now," Lucy said. "Both of us."

And they did.

How to Get Started as a Coder

If you want to learn more about coding, all you need is a computer, access to the Internet, and a parent's permission to use them both. Abundant free resources are available that will let you learn how to code all the projects Lucy and her friends accomplish in their after-school coding camp.

The best place to start is with the Hour of Code website: https://code.org/learn. There you will find an astonishing array of projects (many with helpful tutorials), identified by grade level. These include how to code a dance party, how to send a boat through a maze, how to animate the letters of your name, and how to design your own computer games.

A wealth of options is also available through MIT's free-to-all Scratch coding program. Just go to their website at https://scratch.mit.edu/. Here you can not only create your own stories, games, and animations, but also share them with the entire online community of fellow Scratch creators.

Happy coding!

Acknowledgments

I can't express enough thanks to the children's-book superstars at Holiday House who helped make Lucy's story as starry as could be. Margaret Ferguson is the editor every author dreams of, offering the perfect blend of encouragement and unfailingly insightful critique. Raina Putter and John Simko made sharp-eyed corrections I would have otherwise missed. Kerry Martin created a delightful design for the series.

Grace Zong is the most genius-y of all artistic geniuses! I hug myself with joy every time I look at her illustrations and mega-darling covers for all the After-School Superstars titles.

My superstar agent, Stephen Fraser, has cheered me on for book after book; his steadfast support means so much to me. Writer friends offered critique on crucial drafts: heartfelt thanks to the Writing Roosters (Tracy Abell, Vanessa Appleby, Jennifer Bertman, Laura Perdew, and Jennifer Sims), and to Leslie

O'Kane. I am also beyond grateful to three elementary school teachers for reading the manuscript and providing feedback on the coding instruction—Amy Glendinning, Clarice Howe-Johnson, and Megan Watkins—as well as young coding guru Quinn Reynolds. Of course, any errors that remain are my responsibility alone.

Megan Watkins allowed me to sit in on her coding workshops at Stott Elementary in Arvarda, Colorado, and Stephanie Winiecki welcomed me to her after-school computer club at Boulder Country Day School. I learned so much from both of these stunningly talented teachers. Some of the coding activities for Lucy's camp were inspired by the extremely helpful book *Helping Kids with Coding for Dummies* by Camille McCue and Sarah Guthal. I spent many hours on the Hour of Code website trying out programs myself. Here my computer programmer son, Gregory Wahl, was a great help to his technologically challenged mom.

Most of all, I'm grateful to my unfailingly patient and cheerful eleven-year-old coding tutor, Lorelei Held, who sat next to me for several afternoons showing me how to code a dance party and to draw and animate my own clumsy pictures. I can't imagine how I could have written the book without her. Thank you, Lorelei!

• •
Read on for a sneak peek at more
• •

AFTER-SCHOOL SUPERSTARS FUN!

• • • AFTER-SCHOOL SUPERSTARS • • •

★★ BOOGIE BASS ★★

SIGN LANGUAGE STAR

• • • Claudia Mills ★ pictures by Grace Zong • • •

Boogie Bass lifted his eyebrows, bugged out his eyes, and stretched his mouth into a grin so big it made his cheeks hurt. Maybe now his littlest brother would stop crying.

Bing didn't.

Boogie wiggled his nose. He waggled his fingers in his ears.

Bing cried even harder.

It was all Boogie's fault. He was the one who had left Bing's bedroom door open. The family dog, called Bear because he was as big as a bear, chewed anything left lying on the floor.

Shoes.

Crayons.

Homework.

The remote for the TV.

And now, Bing's little stuffed dog that he carried everywhere. Doggie-Dog no longer had a head, just a small soggy body. Boogie had banished Bear to the kitchen for this terrible crime.

As Bing clutched what was left of Doggie-Dog, Boogie picked him up and held him on his lap. He wrapped his arms around Bing's shaking shoulders.

"What do we do now?" he asked his best friend, Nolan, who had come over to spend a snowy Sunday afternoon hanging out together.

But even Nolan, the smartest kid in the entire third grade at Longwood Elementary, had nothing to offer but a sad shrug.

Boogie's dad was at work. He was a plumber. "Toilets don't just overflow on weekdays," was one of his dad's sayings. His mom was in bed with a migraine headache. Boogie knew better than to bother her unless someone was dripping blood on the carpet.

As Bing continued to sob on Boogie's lap, his other two brothers raced into the living room, the bigger one chasing the smaller one and both screaming at the top of their lungs.

"I'm going to get you!" T.J. shouted.

"Nooooo!" shrieked Gib, his shirt left behind somewhere—probably being chewed right this minute by Bear.

All four brothers had fancy names. Their mother, who was generally a very unfancy person, liked names that sounded elegant. But they had all ended up with unfancy nicknames. Nine-year-old Boogie's real name was Brewster. Six-year-old T.J.'s real name was Truman James. Four-year-old Gib's real name was Gibson. And two-year-old Bing's real name was Bingley.

"What's wrong with him this time?" T.J. asked, giving up the chase to point at Bing.

"Bear ate Doggie-Dog's head," Boogie explained.

T.J. burst out laughing. Gib, who copied everything T.J. did, laughed even harder.

"It's not funny!" Boogie told them. Except it would have been, if poor Bing wasn't crying so hard.

Boogie had to think of something to make Bing stop crying. He looked at the flakes swirling outside the window and the thick layer of snow already frosting the yard.

"Let's go sledding!"

Nolan shook his head. Boogie suddenly remembered the work it would be to dig up four snow jackets, four pairs of snow pants, four pairs of snow boots, four pairs of snow mittens, and four snow hats, plus stuff for Nolan, too.

"Let's go *indoor* sledding!" Boogie said. "The stairs can be the Olympic sledding course. No, the Olympic *luge* course. We can use the laundry basket for the luge."

Nolan shook his head again, but T.J. had already dashed into the laundry room and returned with a large plastic tub.

"There was some stuff in it, but I didn't know if it was clean or dirty, so I dumped it out on the floor," T.J. said. "Don't worry, I closed the laundry room door so Bear can't get in there to chew it. Or at least I think I did."

The next thing Boogie knew, T.J. and Gib were sitting in the laundry basket at the top of the stairs.

"Give us a push!" T.J. called to Boogie and Nolan.

"I don't think your mom is going to like this," Nolan said to Boogie. But Boogie couldn't disappoint the others now. He set Bing down on the couch, climbed up the stairs, and gave the laundry basket a hard shove.

Down the stairs it clattered, riders screaming, Bear howling from the kitchen, where he knew he was missing out on all the fun.

"Gold medal!" T.J. shouted as they crashed into the back of the couch.

"Again!" Gib shouted. "Go fast again!"

After the second crash-landing, T.J. pumped his fist into the air. "Is there something even better than a gold medal? Like a chocolate-covered gold medal?"

"Again!" Gib continued to shout.

At least Bing had stopped crying. But Boogie saw Bing looking toward the laundry basket with longing in his eyes. Quiet little Bing hardly ever got a turn at anything.

"It's Bing's turn," Boogie announced.

"Awww!!" T.J. and Gib complained.

"It's *Bing's* turn," Boogie repeated.

Boogie carried the laundry basket back up the stairs and helped Bing, who was still clutching Doggie-Dog, climb into it.

"Ready?" he asked.

Bing pointed at Boogie, then at the basket. Bing hadn't started talking very much yet.

"You want me to get in with you?" Boogie asked. "Okay, here we go!"

Just as he shoved off, from the corner of his eye, Boogie saw Nolan frantically drawing a line across his neck with his finger, clearly the sign for *Disaster heading your way RIGHT NOW!*

Behind Nolan stood Boogie's mother.

But it was too late to stop anything.

Down went the sled, sailing past the couch this time into a narrow table, where a vase stood full of flowers.

Crash!

Where a vase *used* to stand, and *used* to be full of flowers.

Water splattered. Shattered pieces of glass flew everywhere. One of them hit Bing in the

cheek, and he began crying again.

"Brewster Bartholomew Bass!" thundered his mother. "What on earth are you doing?"

"Um—indoor luge?"

"And whose idea was this?"

"Um—mine?"

"Oh, Boogie." Now his mother looked close to tears, too. "And they say the oldest child is supposed to be the *responsible* one. Boogie, all I wanted was one hour of peace and quiet. Not one hour of indoor luge!" She turned to Nolan. "Tell me, do *you* organize indoor Olympic winter sports at *your* house? Never mind, I know the answer to *that* one."

Nolan had already retrieved a towel, broom, and dustpan from the kitchen and was sopping up the spilled water and sweeping up the vase pieces. He spent so much time at Boogie's house he could find whatever was needed even better than the people who lived there.

Just then Boogie's mother's eyes fell upon the headless body of a certain stuffed dog that had fallen out of the laundry-basket-luge when it crashed.

"Oh, no," she said. "What happened here?"

"I left Bing's bedroom door open," Boogie muttered.

"Oh, Boogie! Nolan, in *your* house, do people forget to follow *very* simple instructions about *very* simple things like closing doors? Never mind, I know the answer to that one, too."

Boogie's mother was right.

Nolan would never think up anything as dumb as indoor luge. And Nolan would never have forgotten to keep Doggie-Dog safe from Bear.

If Nolan had been the oldest brother in Boogie's family, Bing wouldn't be in tears right now.

Boogie had always been proud to have a friend as smart as Nolan. In the after-school program they attended together, Nolan had been the best at chopping and measuring in cooking camp. In comic-book camp, Nolan had known tons of cool facts about the history of comics. In coding camp, Nolan had been the coding wizard. Boogie hadn't been very good at cooking, or drawing, *or* coding. Actually, he had been pretty terrible at all of them, but the camps had always been tons of fun.

Now they were starting a four-week sign-language camp on Monday. Boogie would bet a hundred chocolate-covered gold medals that Nolan would be really good at sign language, and a hundred times better at it than he was.

Nolan was better at *everything* than Boogie was, even better at being a brother.

"Boogie, do you ever hear *anything* I say?" his mother asked.

It was clear his mother didn't expect him to give a reply.

So Boogie helped Nolan with the sweeping as his mother carried Bing off to get a Band-Aid, leaving Doggie-Dog's headless body behind on the floor.

Maybe in sign-language camp they'd start out by learning the sign for *I'm sorry*. Right now, that would be a very useful thing for Boogie to know.

Right now, he was sorry about everything.

Claudia Mills is the acclaimed author of more than sixty books for children, including the Franklin School Friends series and the middle-grade novel *Zero Tolerance*. She recently received the Kerlan Award. She lives in Boulder, Colorado.

Grace Zong has illustrated many books for children, including *Goldy Luck and the Three Pandas* by Natasha Yim and *Mrs. McBee Leaves Room 3* by Gretchen Brandenburg McLellan. She divides her time between South Korea and New York.